# IT'S NOT EASY BEING A
# SUPERHERO

by
Kelli Call

illustrated by
Tony Pham

## Understanding Sensory Processing Disorder

pink umbrella
books

To my son, Clark. Thanks for teaching me what it means to be a superhero.

Published by Pink Umbrella Books (www.pinkumbrellapublishing.com)

It's Not Easy Being a Superhero/ Kelli Call
  Clark learns to defeat sensory triggers one superpower at a time.
ISBN: 978-1949598025
Library of Congress Control Number: 2018965946
Edited by Merry Gordon and Marnae Kelley
Illustrations by Tony Pham
Illustration © 2019 Tony Pham

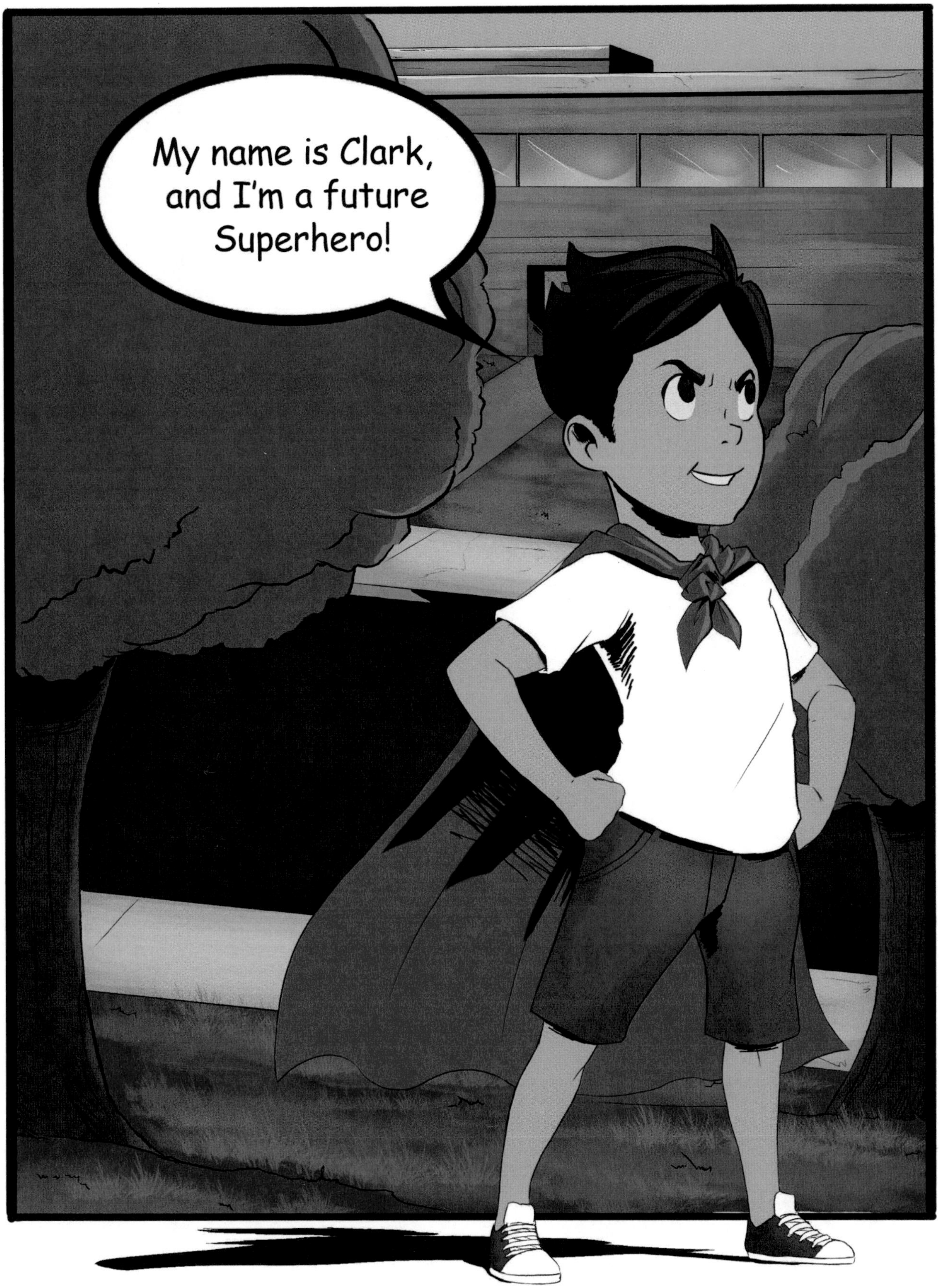
My name is Clark, and I'm a future Superhero!

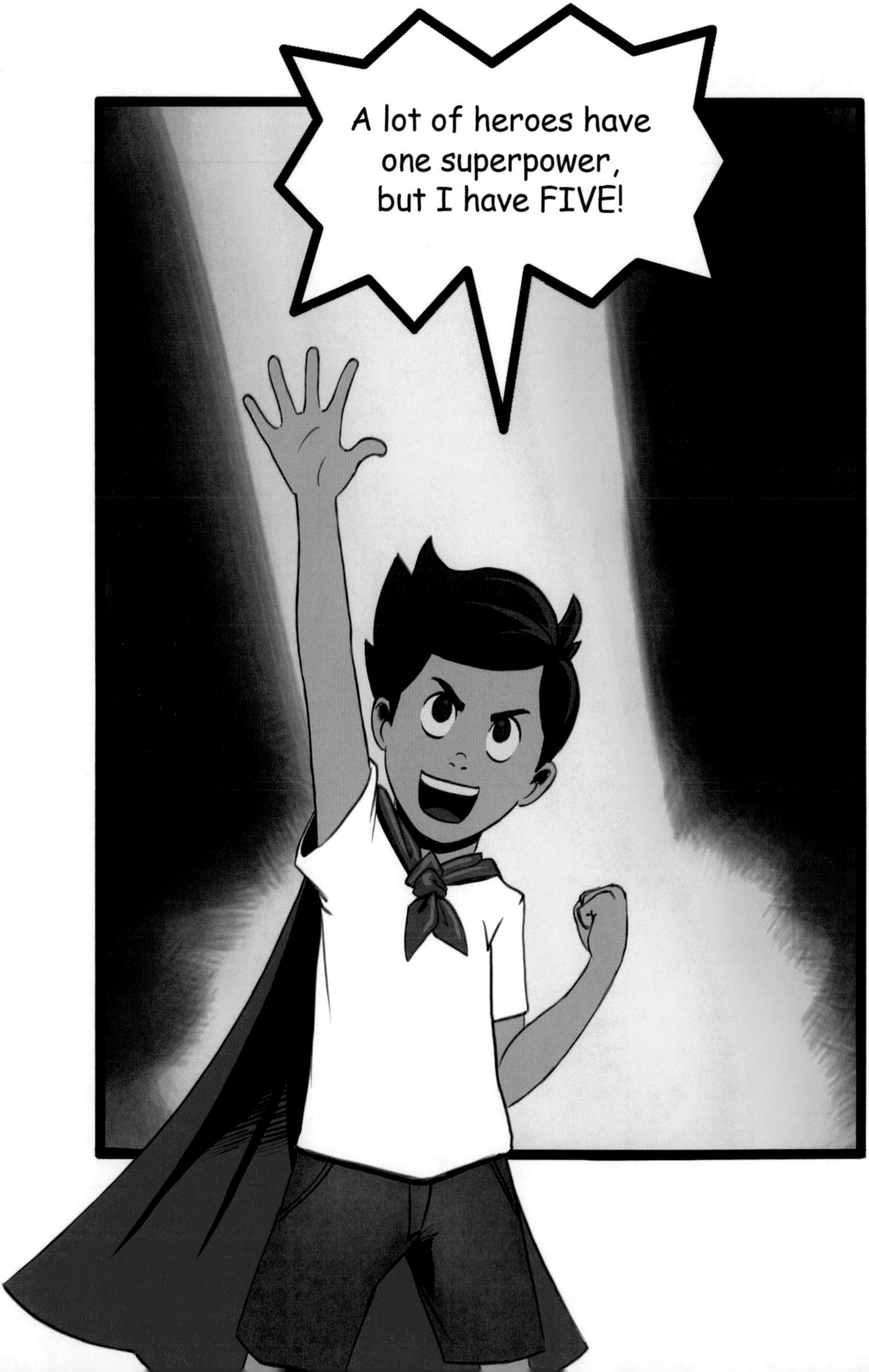
A lot of heroes have one superpower, but I have FIVE!

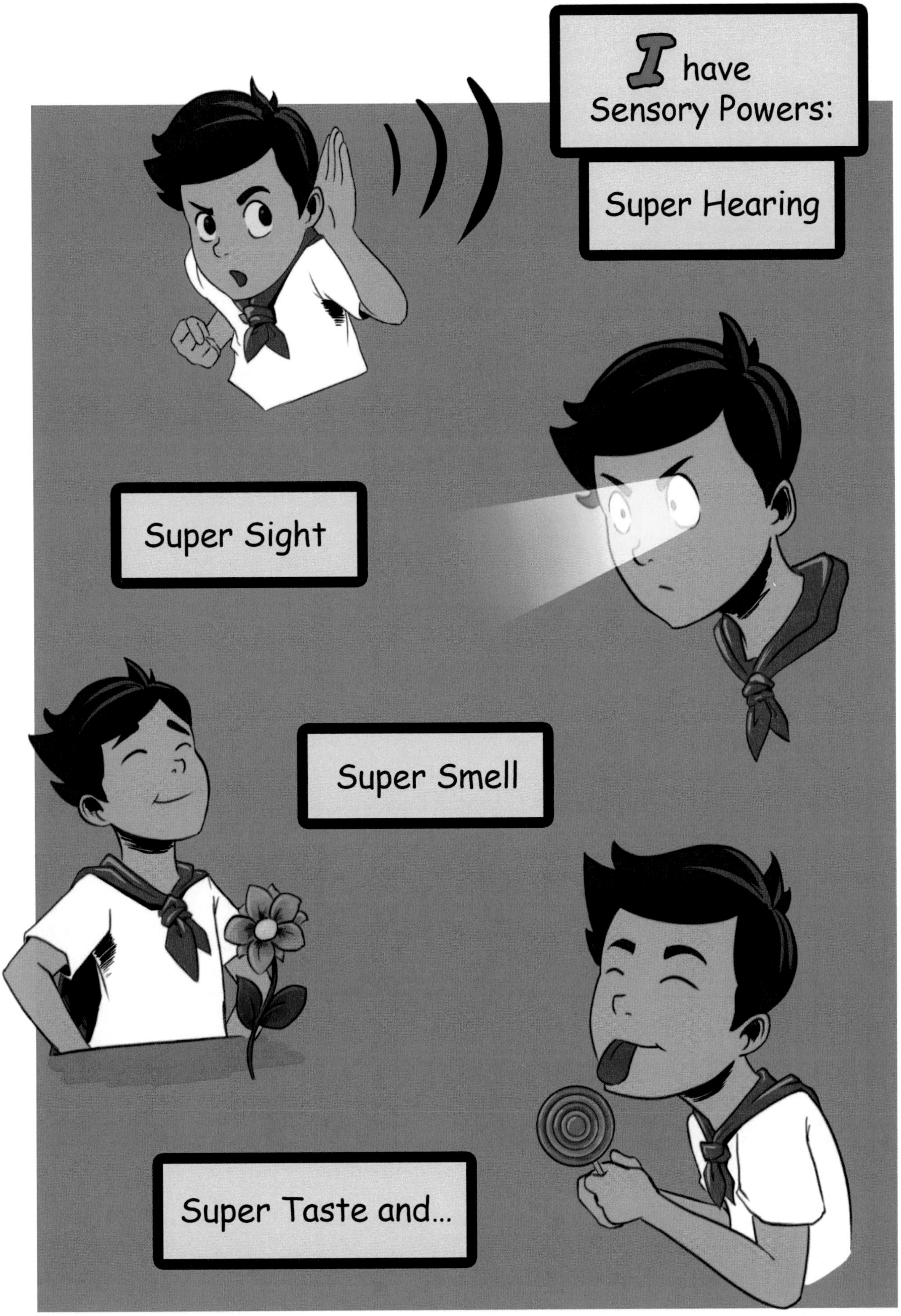
I have Sensory Powers:
Super Hearing
Super Sight
Super Smell
Super Taste and...

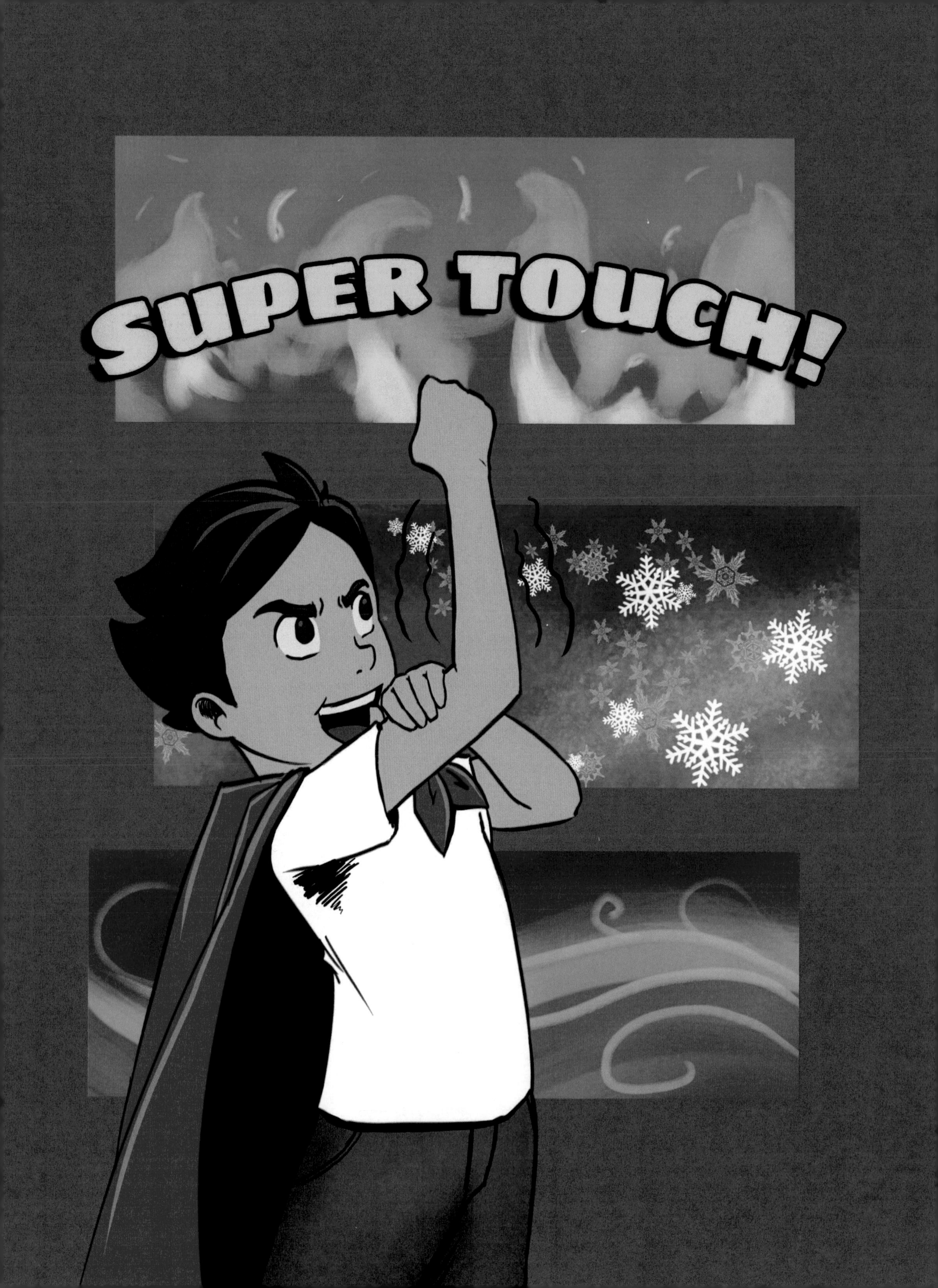
SUPER TOUCH!

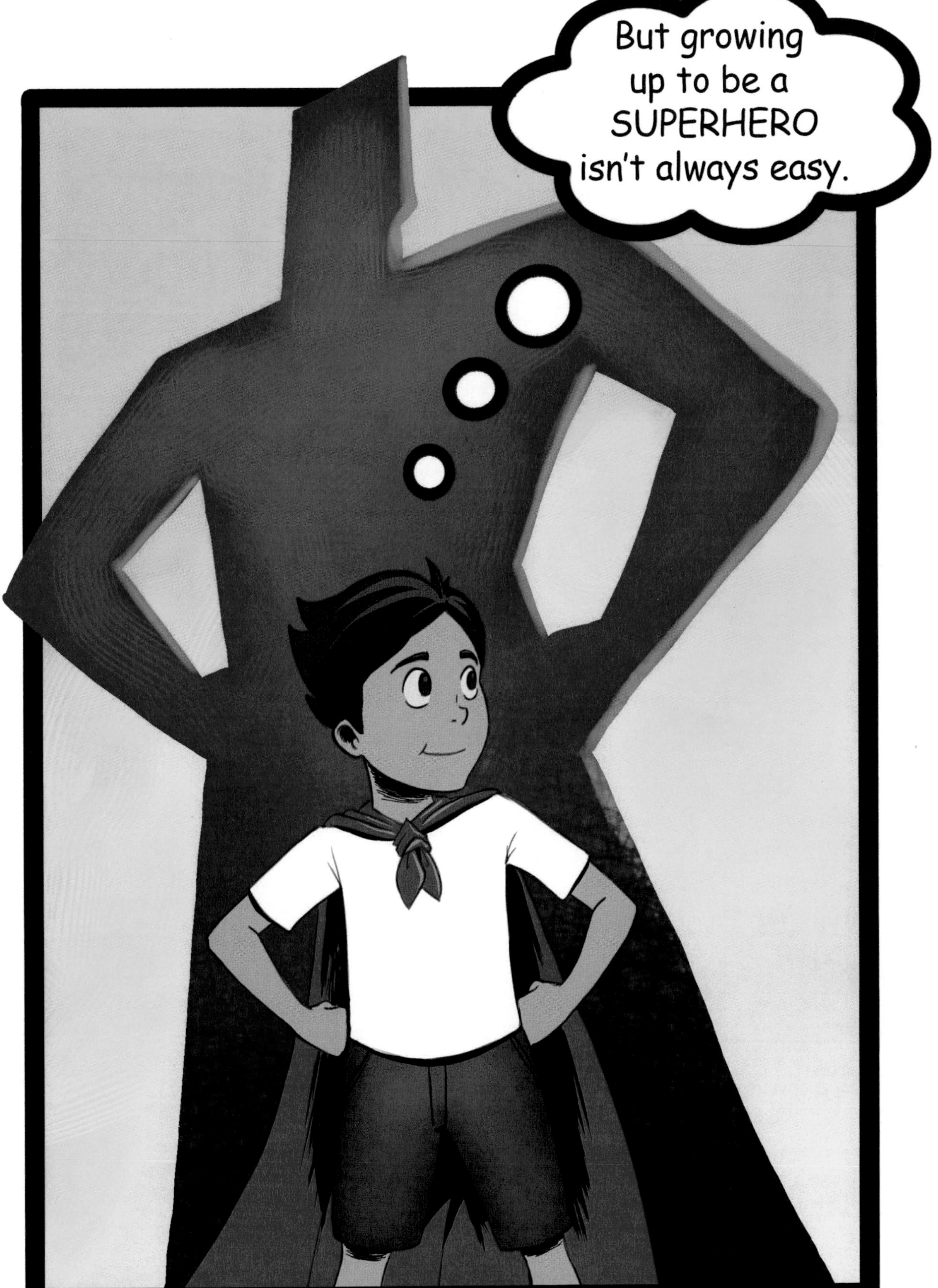
But growing up to be a SUPERHERO isn't always easy.

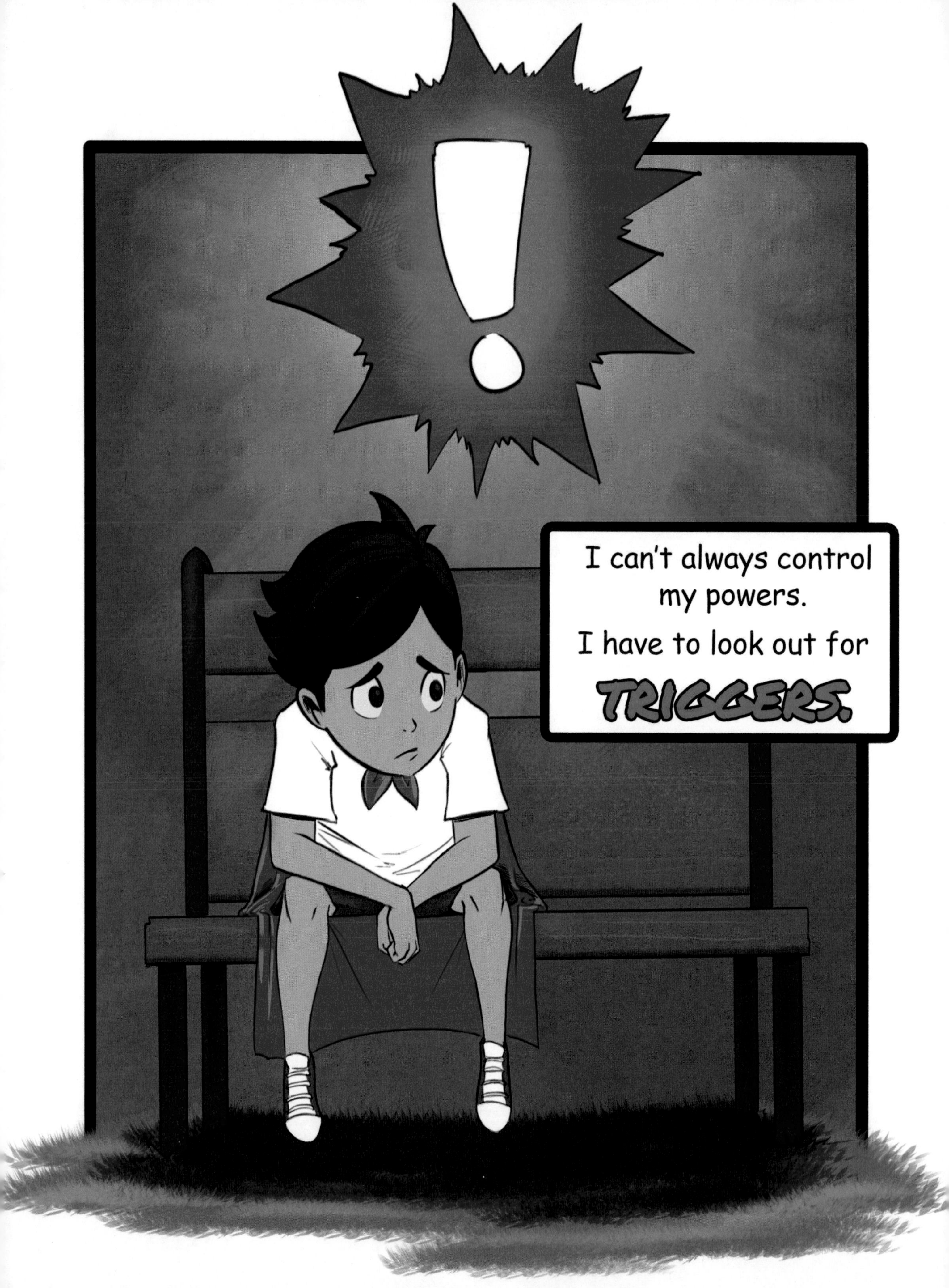
I can't always control my powers.
I have to look out for
TRIGGERS.

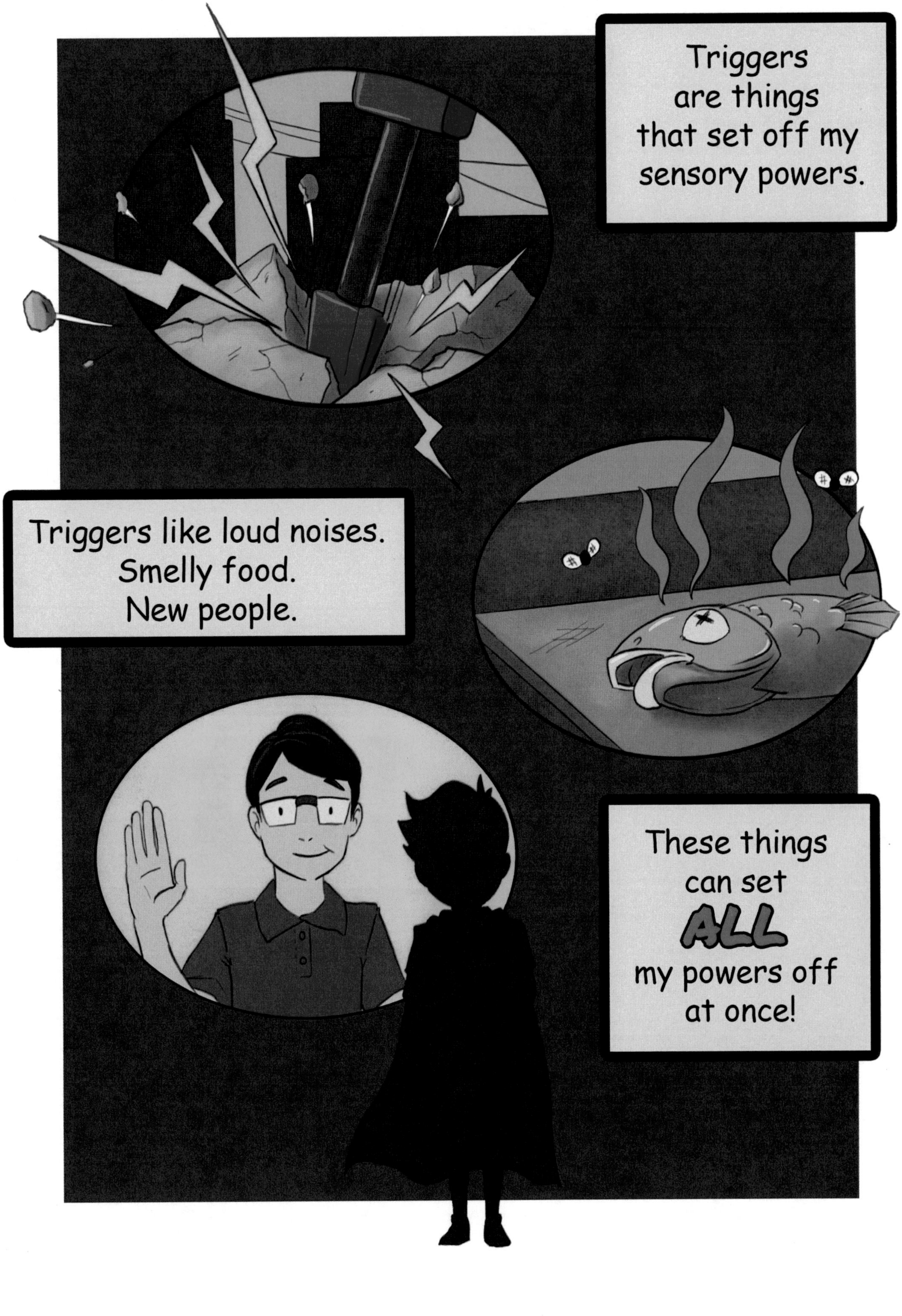
Triggers are things that set off my sensory powers.
Triggers like loud noises. Smelly food. New people.
These things can set ALL my powers off at once!

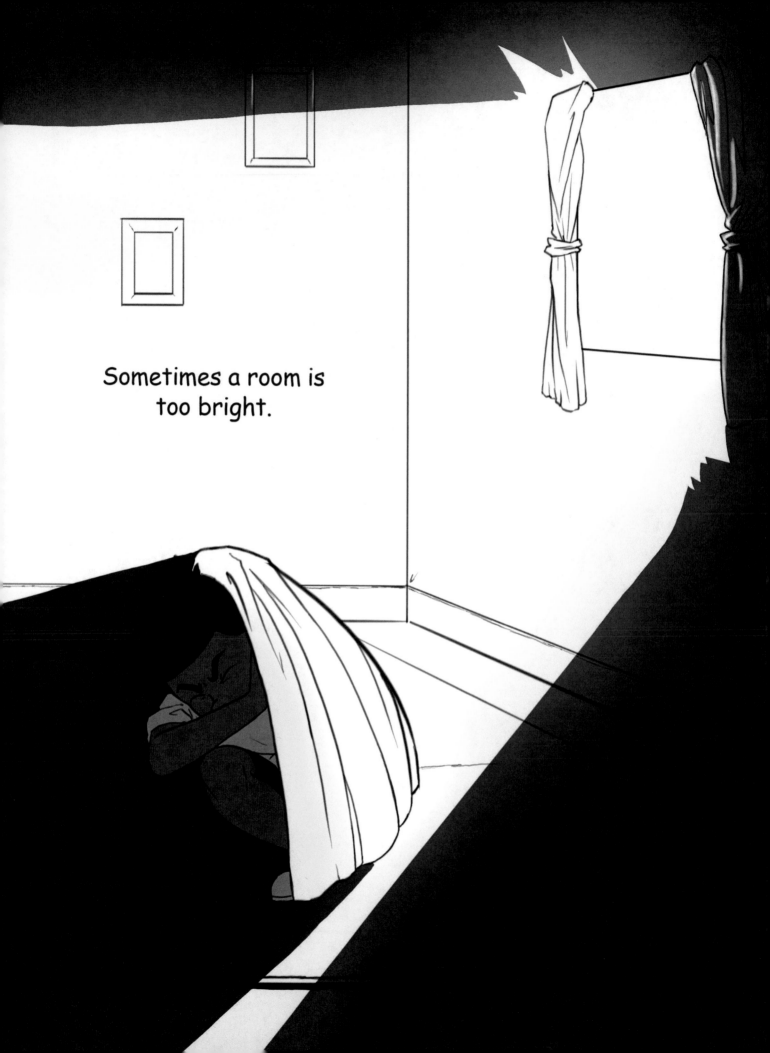

Sometimes a room is too bright.

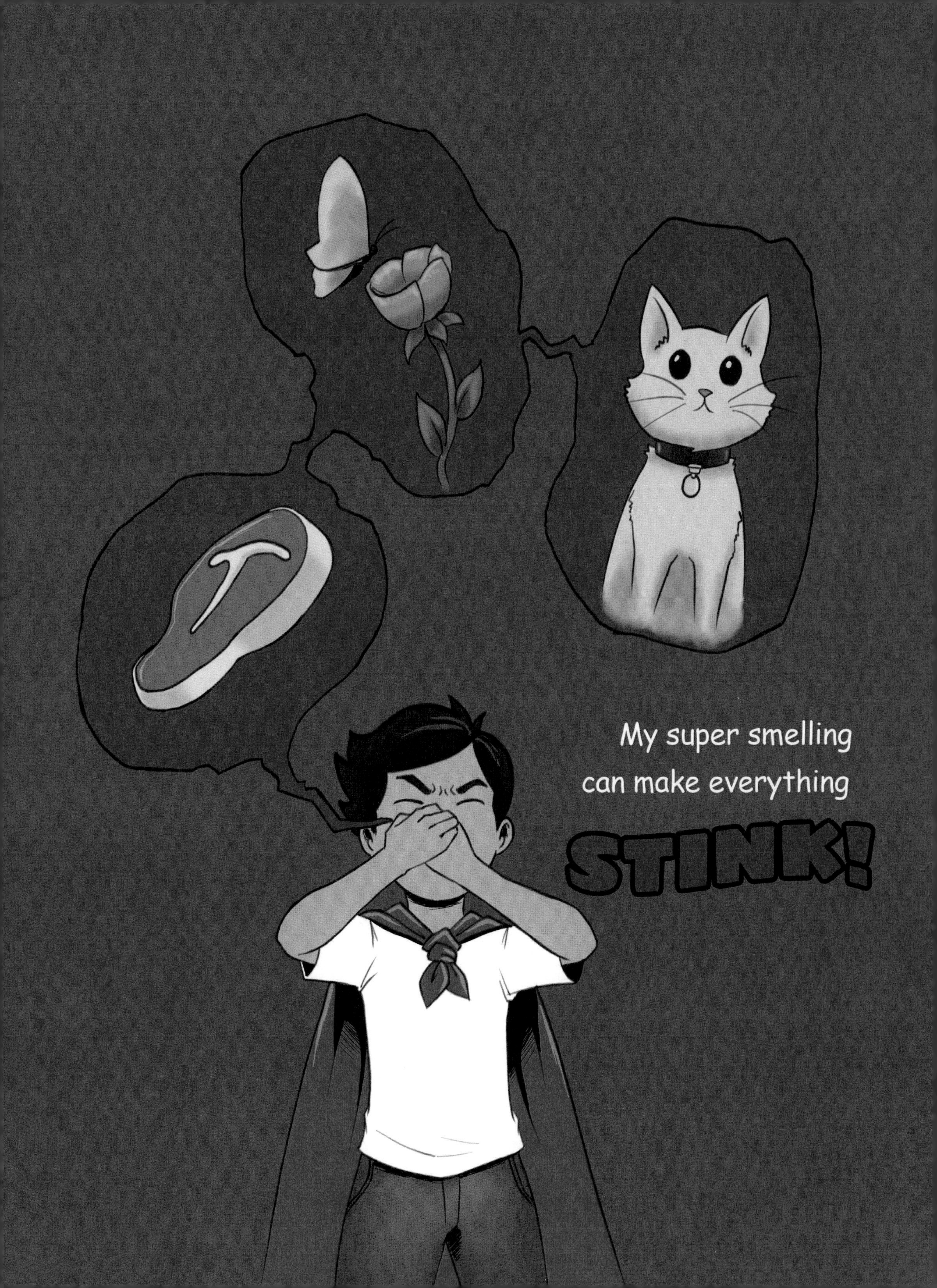
My super smelling
can make everything
STINK!

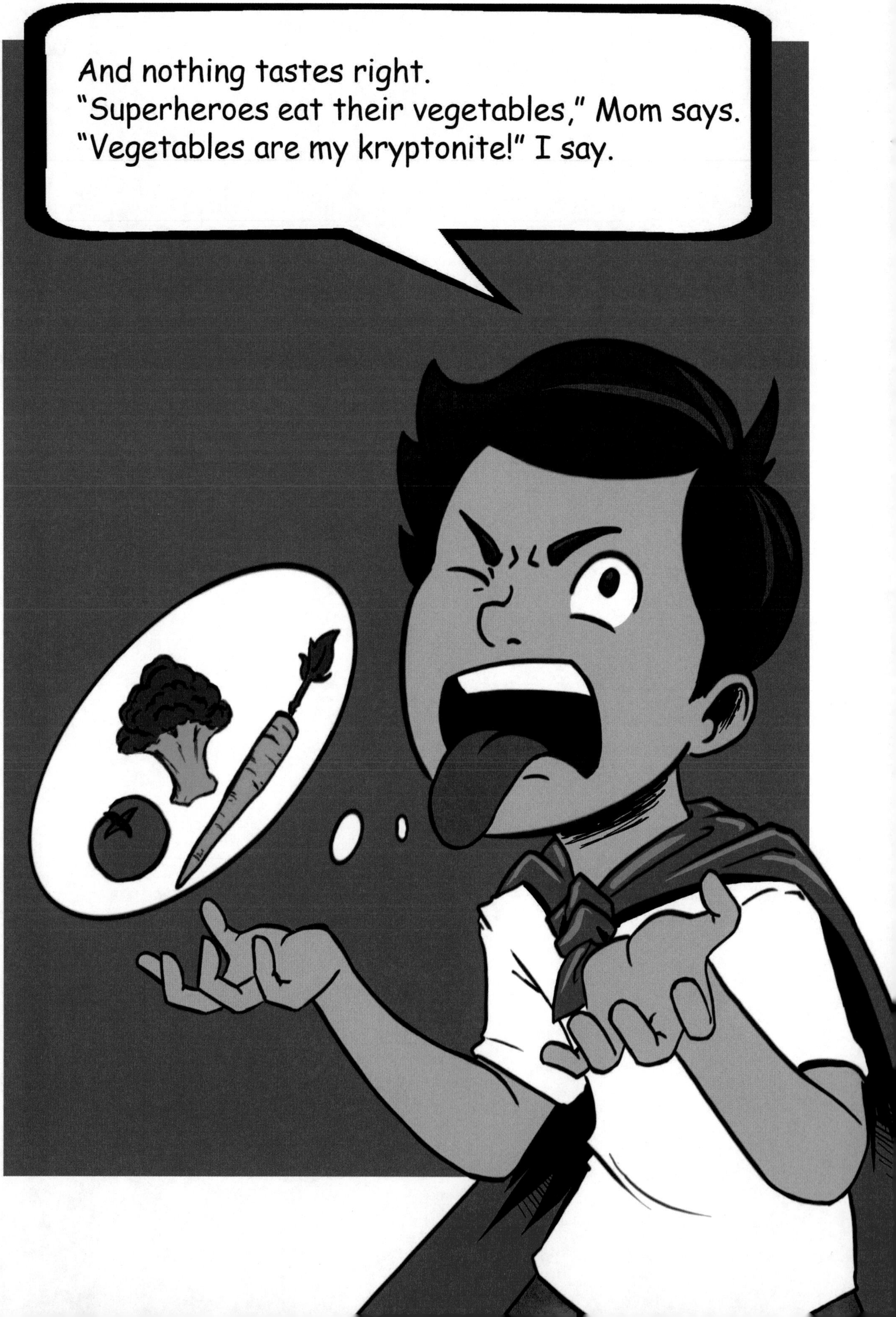
And nothing tastes right.
"Superheroes eat their vegetables," Mom says.
"Vegetables are my kryptonite!" I say.

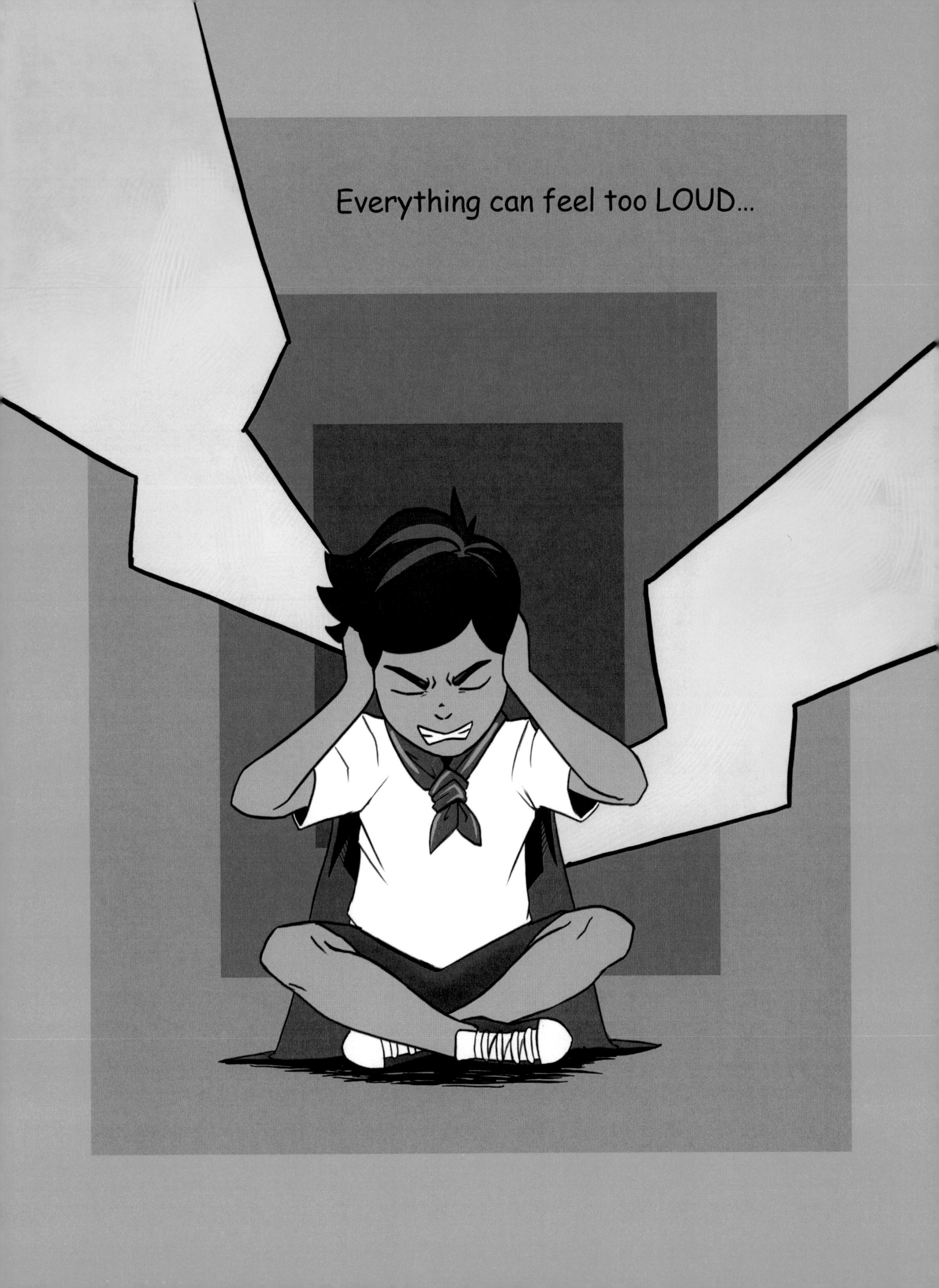
Everything can feel too LOUD...

Or too quiet.

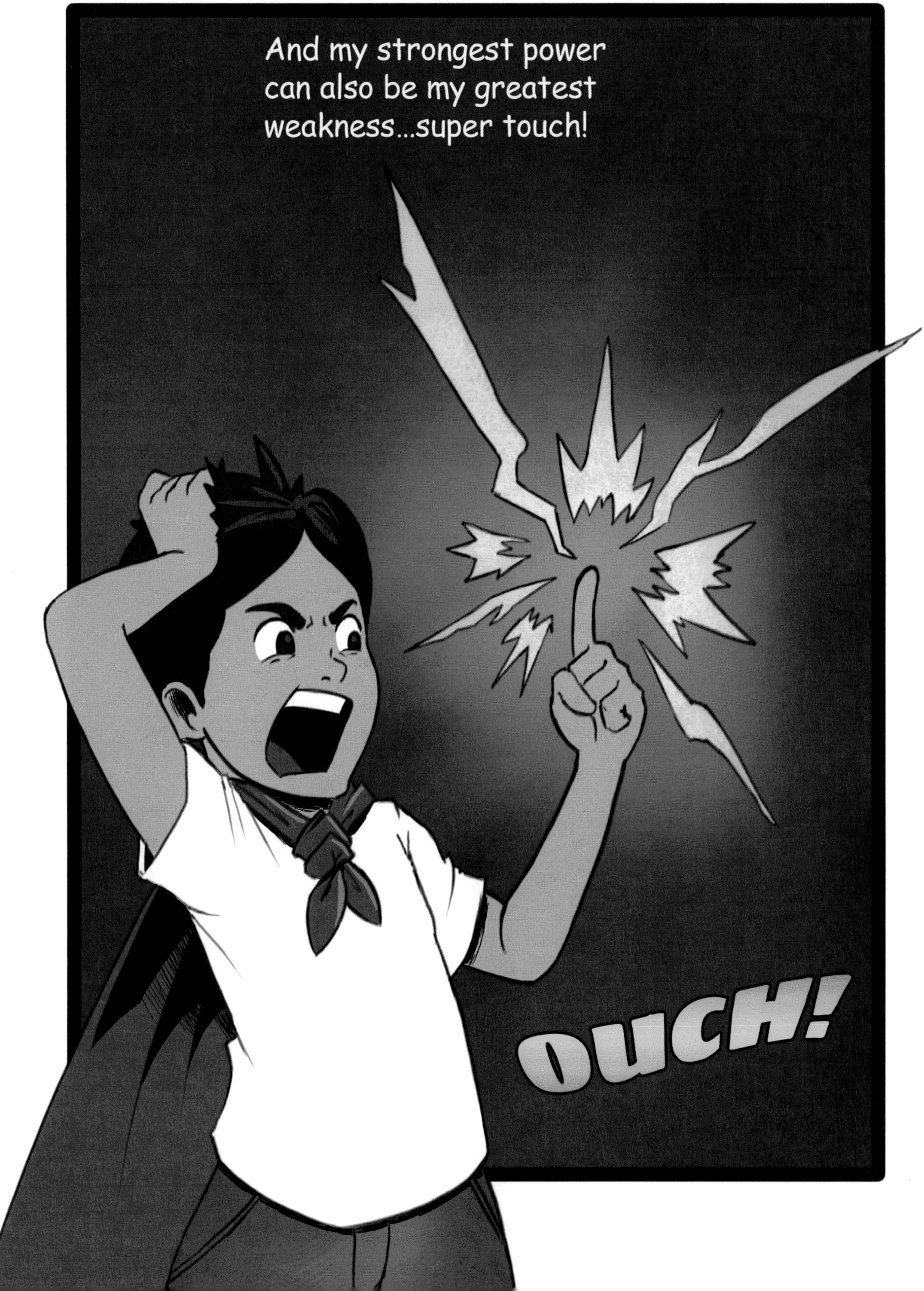
And my strongest power can also be my greatest weakness...super touch!
OUCH!

I can play in the cold or heat for a long time
and my sensory powers keep me from feeling it.

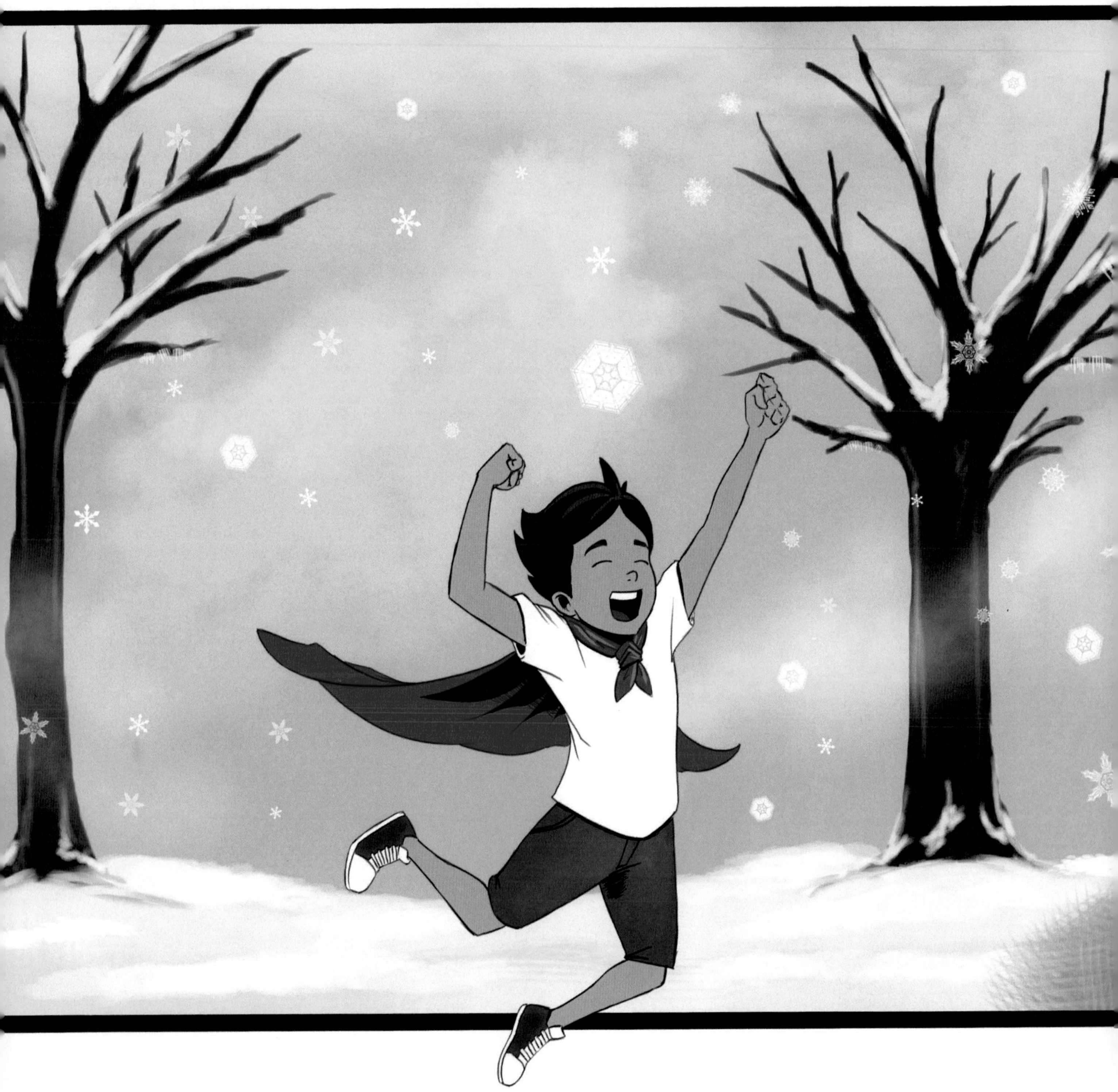

But that isn't always a good thing.

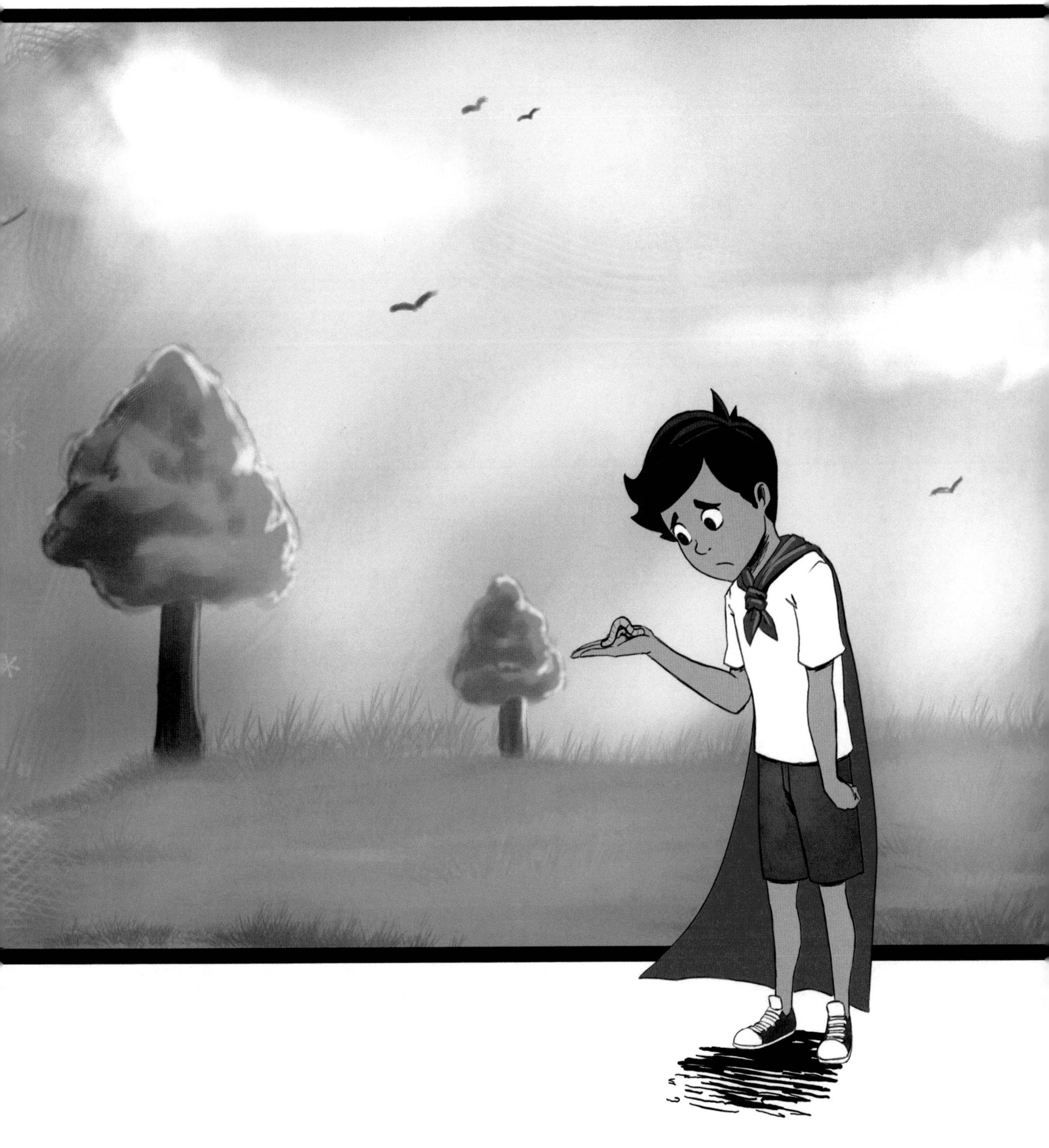

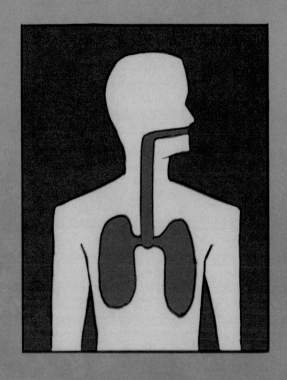

Like other
superheroes,
I have sidekicks.

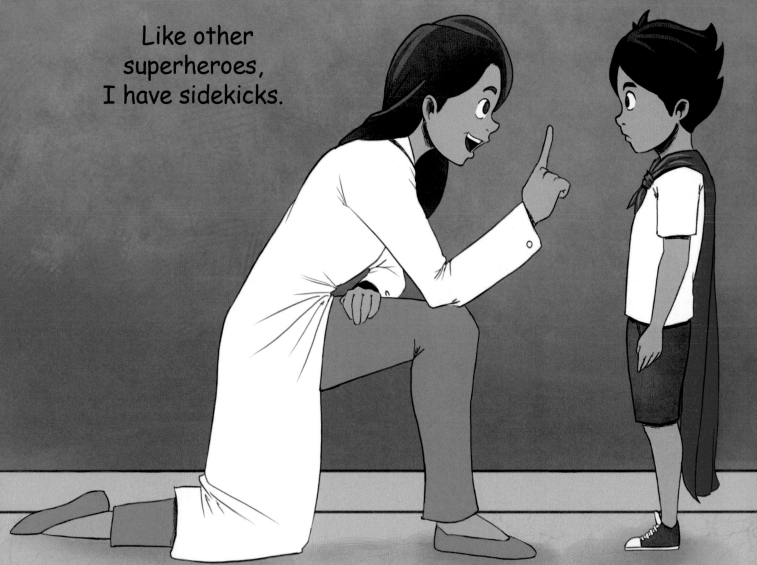

My sidekicks teach me the tricks to
controlling my powers.

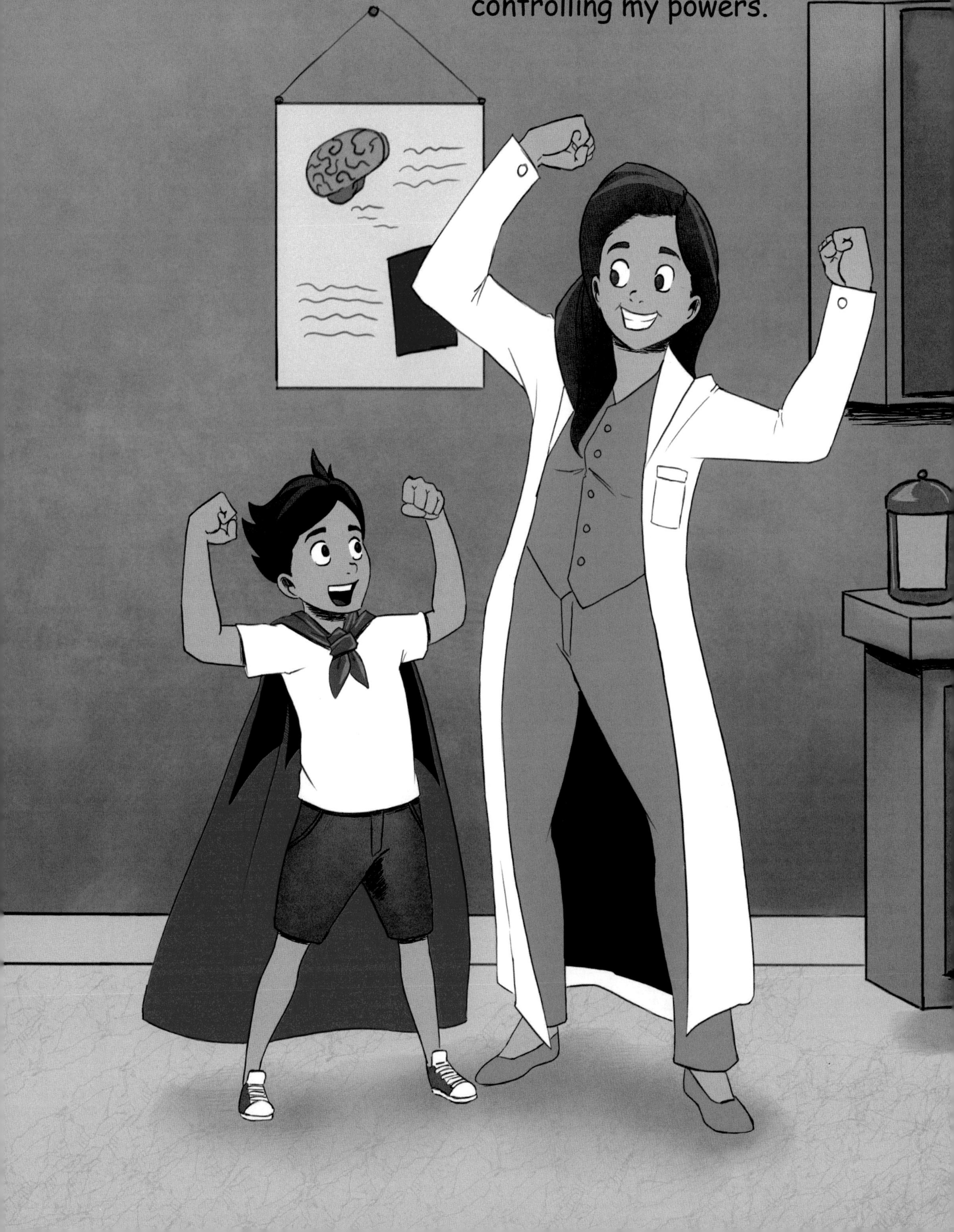

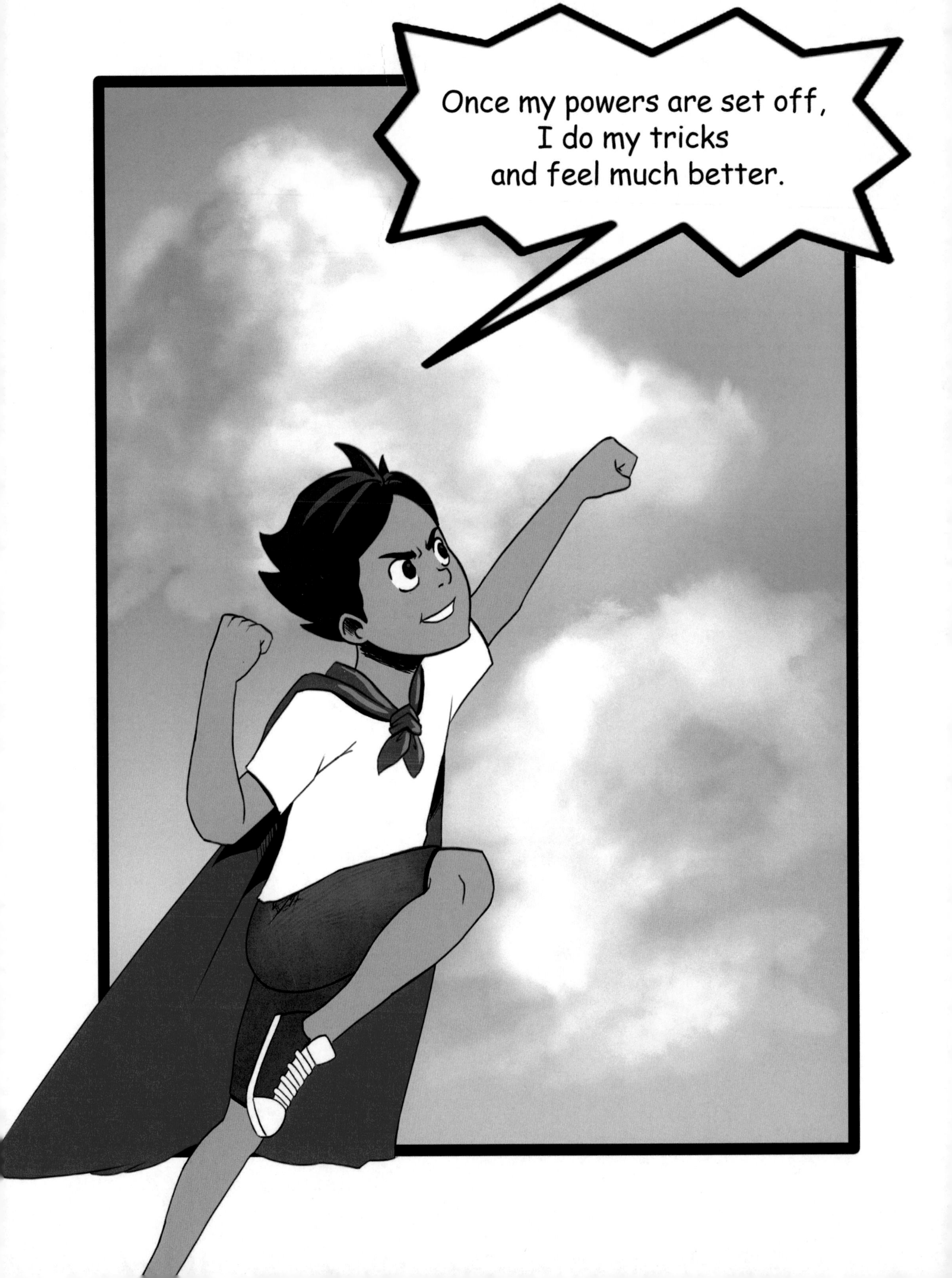
Once my powers are set off, I do my tricks and feel much better.

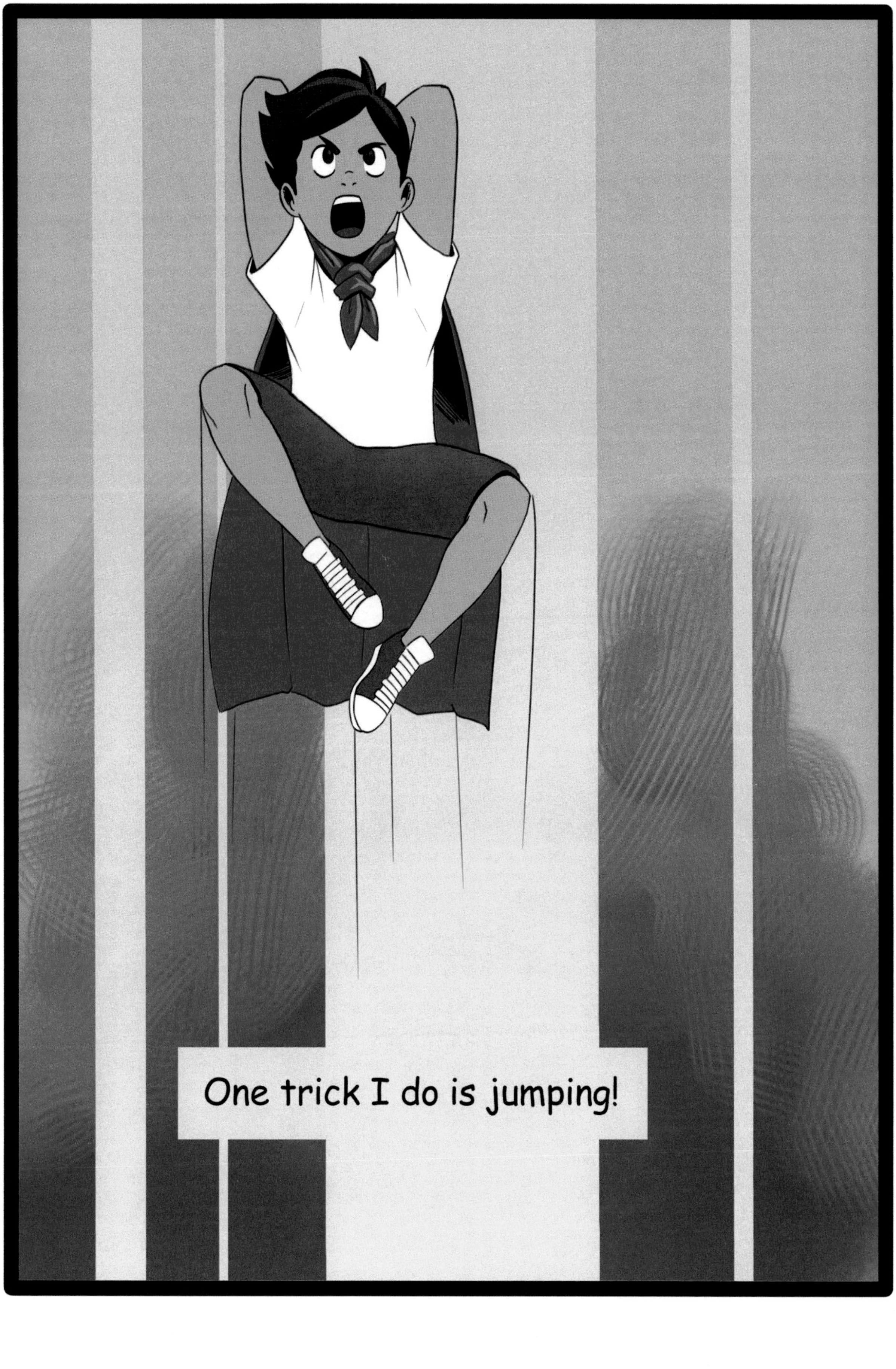
One trick I do is jumping!

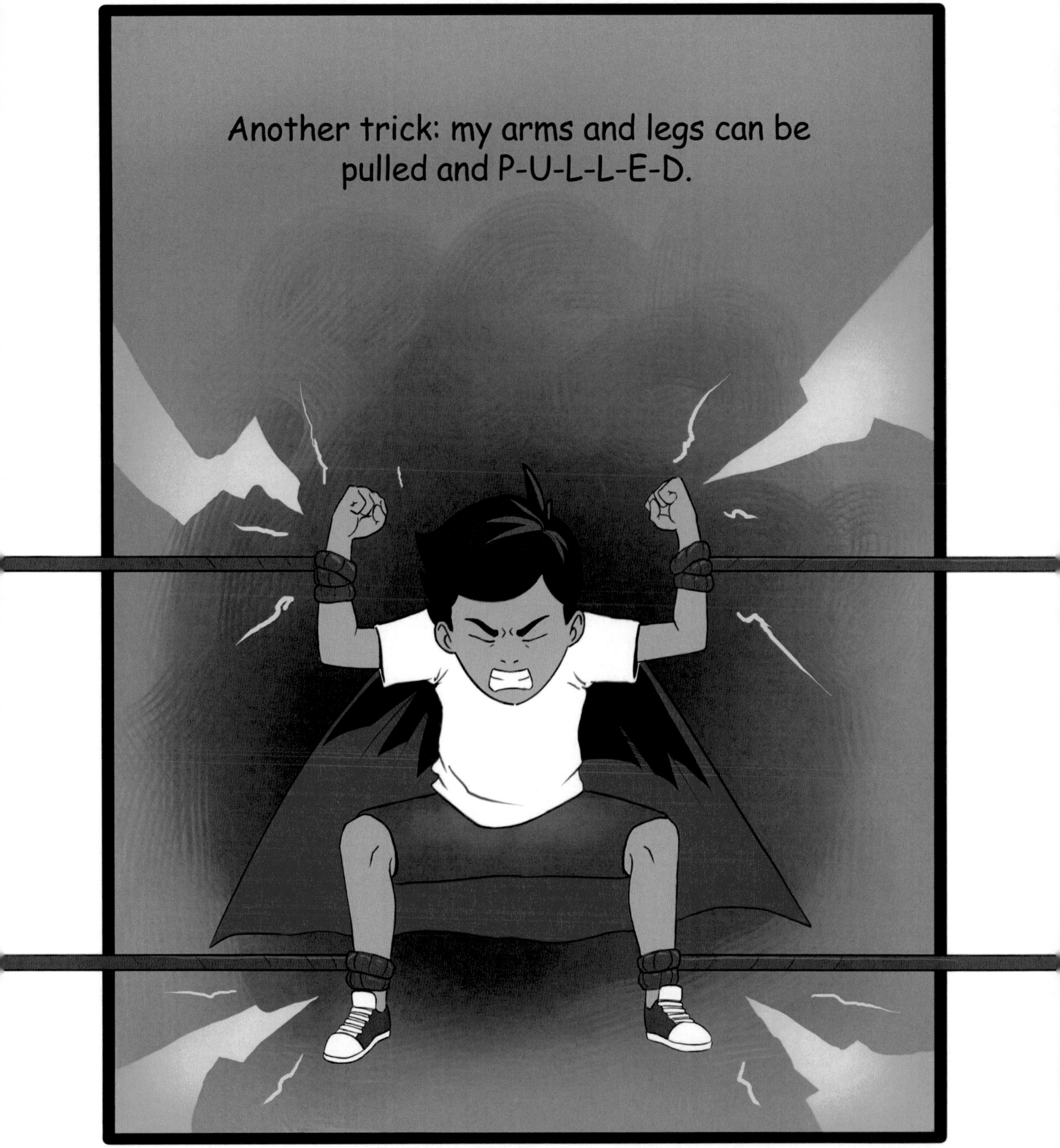
Another trick: my arms and legs can be pulled and P-U-L-L-E-D.

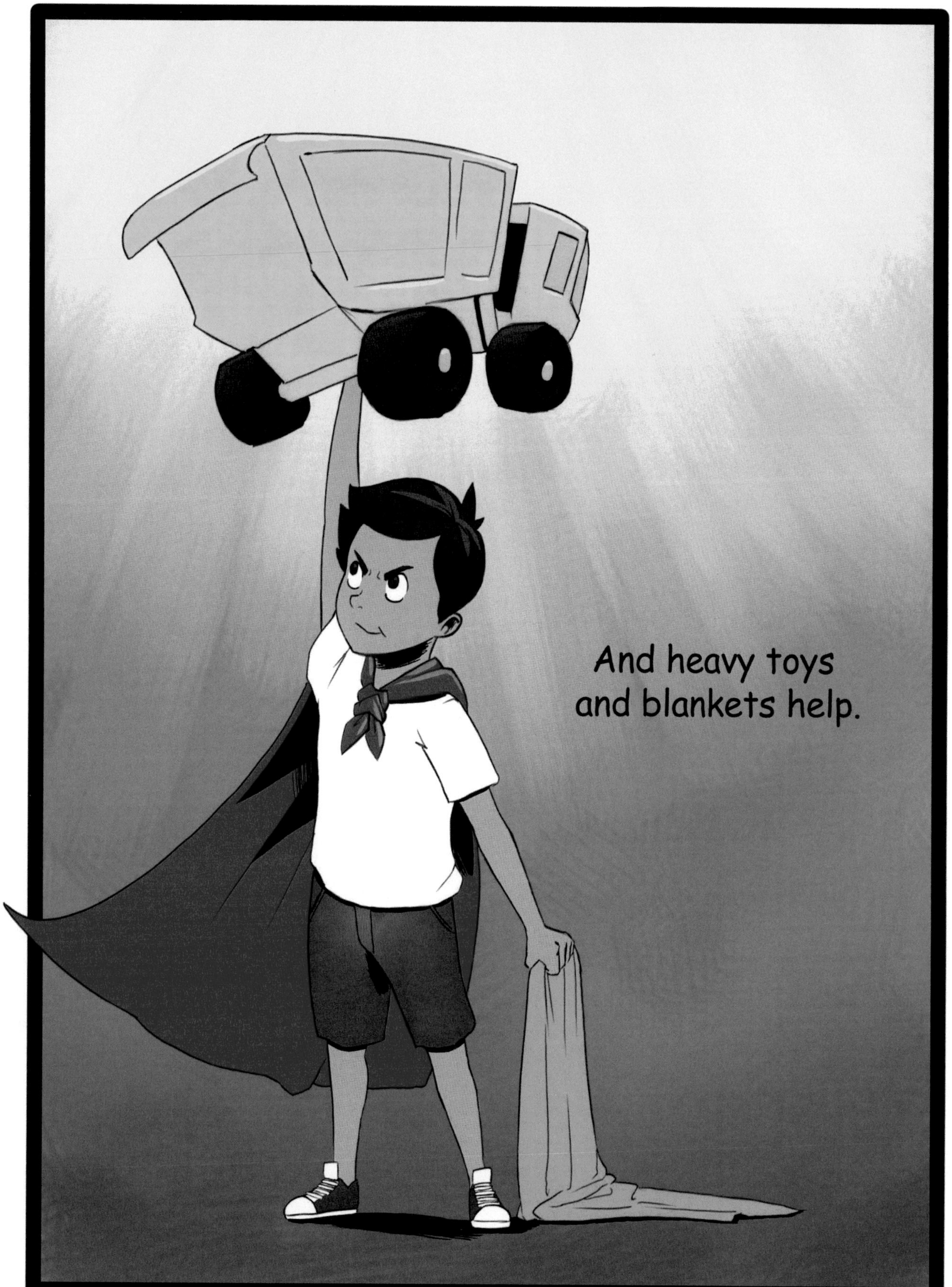
And heavy toys and blankets help.

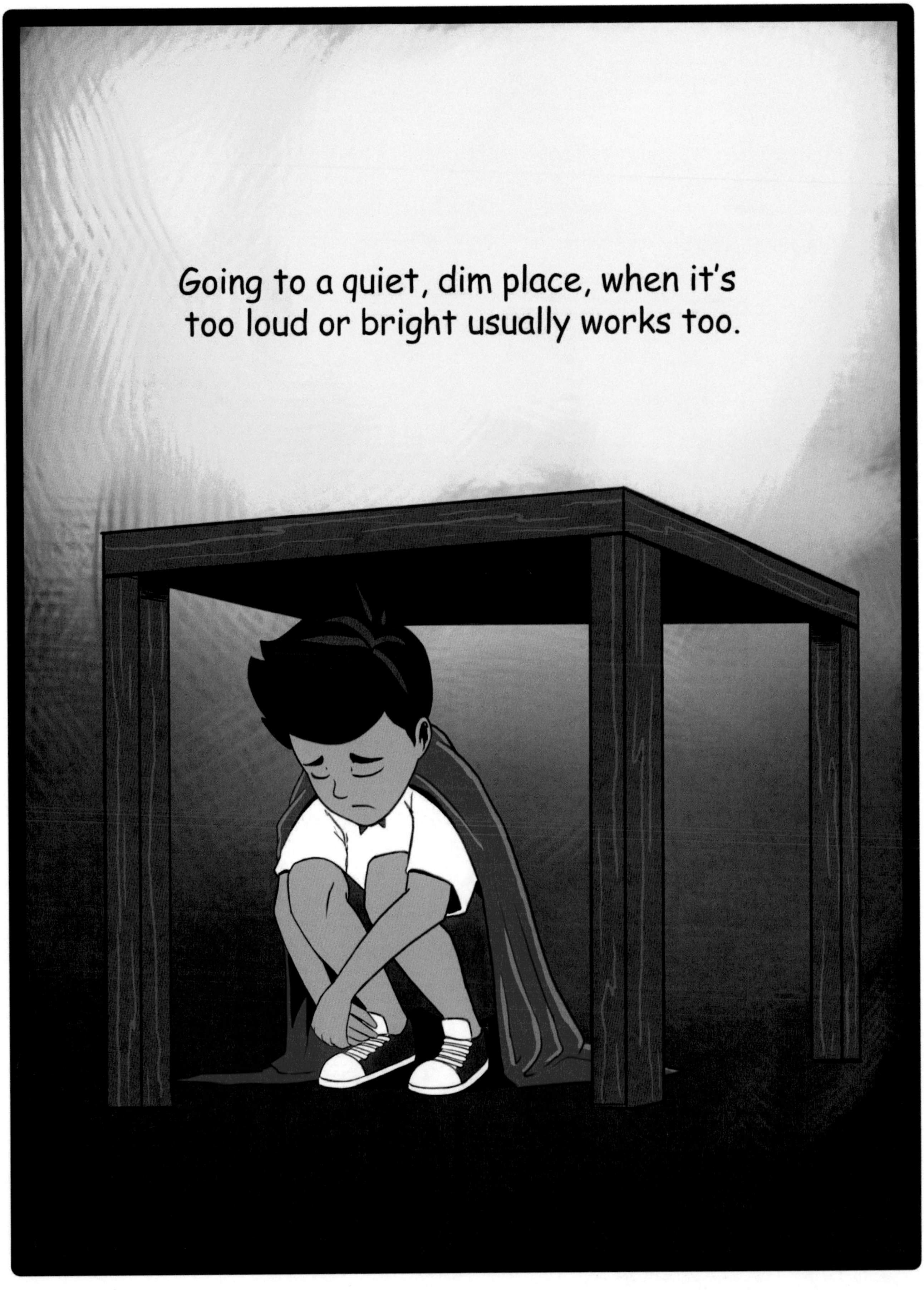
Going to a quiet, dim place, when it's too loud or bright usually works too.

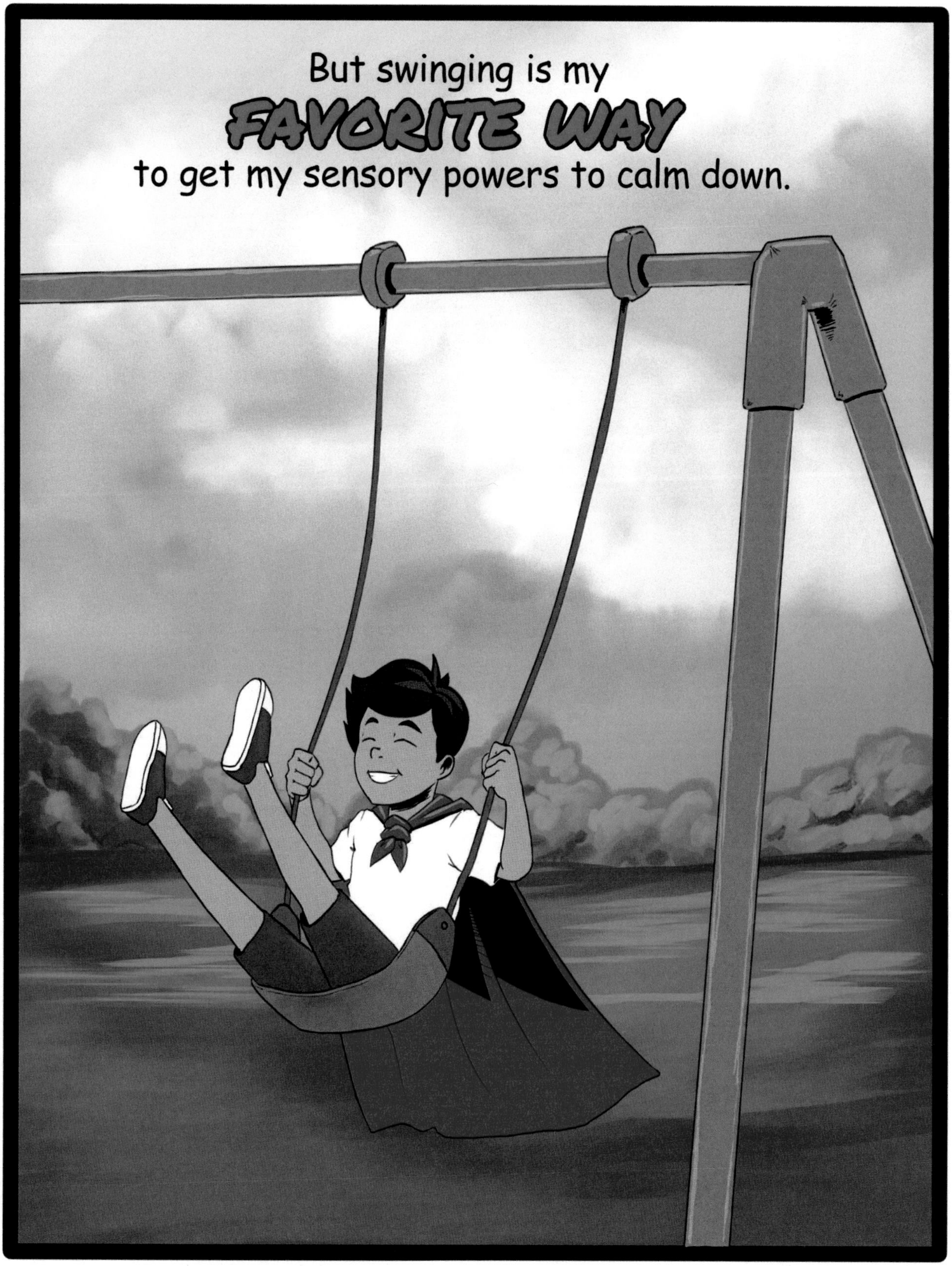
But swinging is my
FAVORITE WAY
to get my sensory powers to calm down.

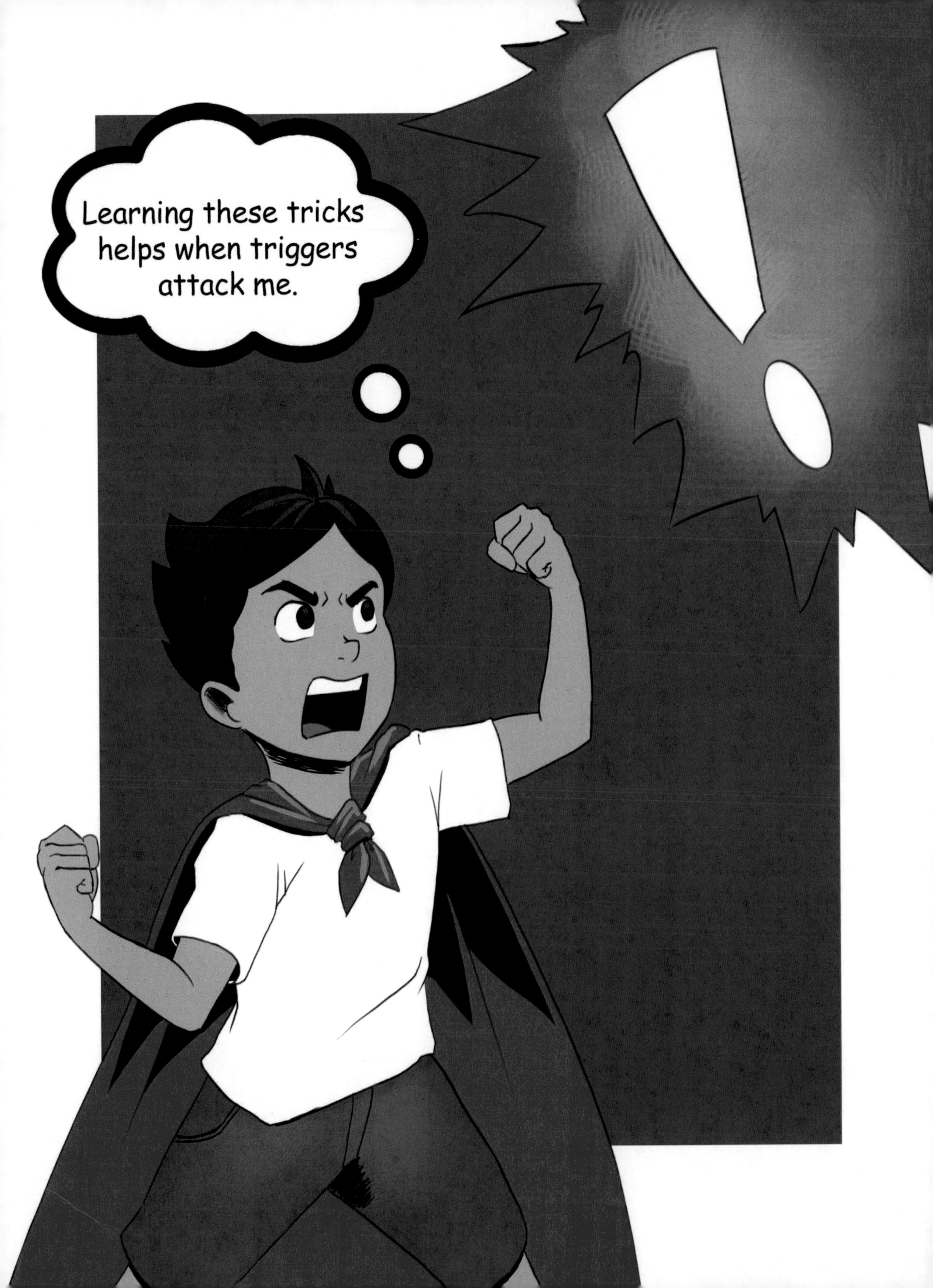
Learning these tricks helps when triggers attack me.

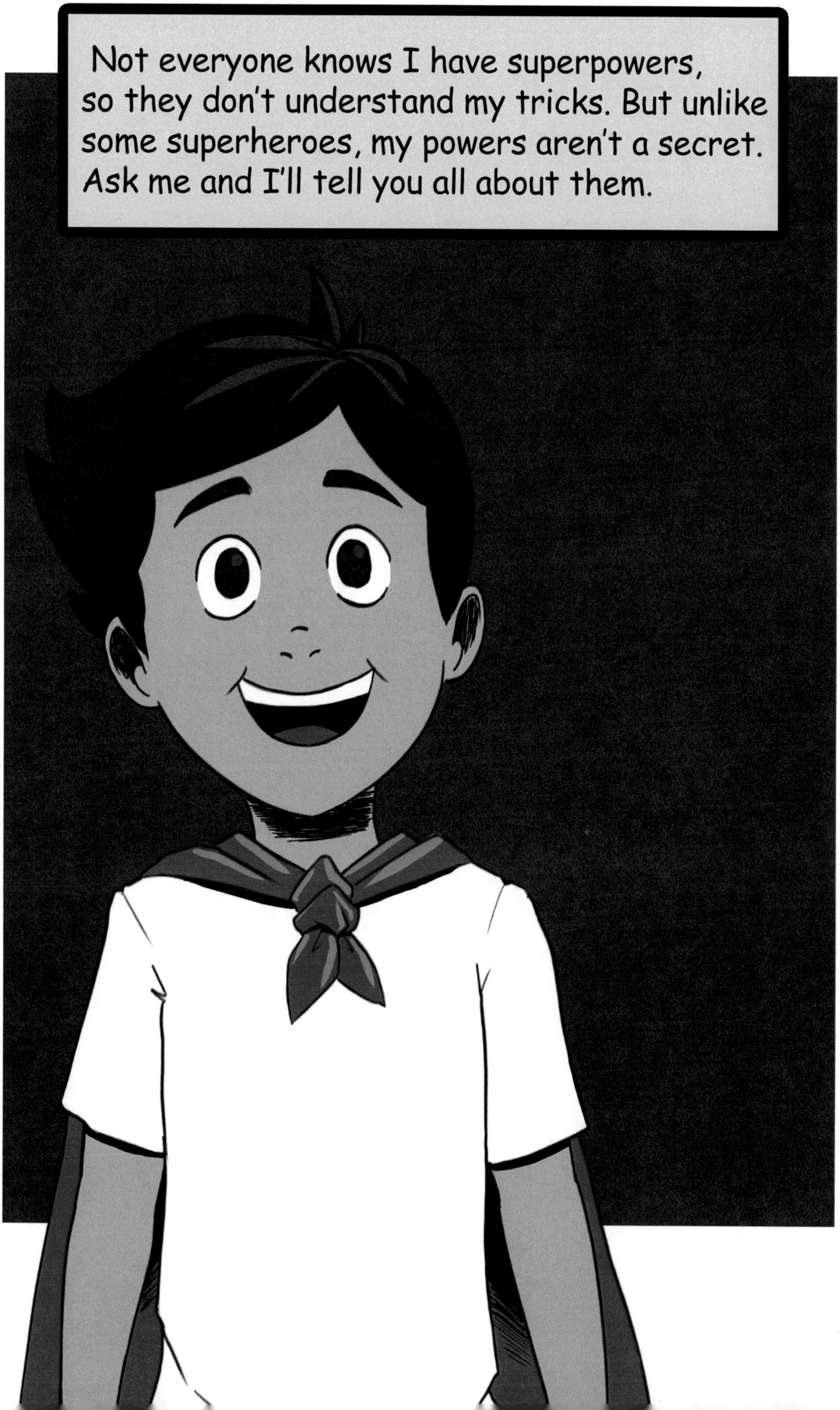
Not everyone knows I have superpowers, so they don't understand my tricks. But unlike some superheroes, my powers aren't a secret. Ask me and I'll tell you all about them.

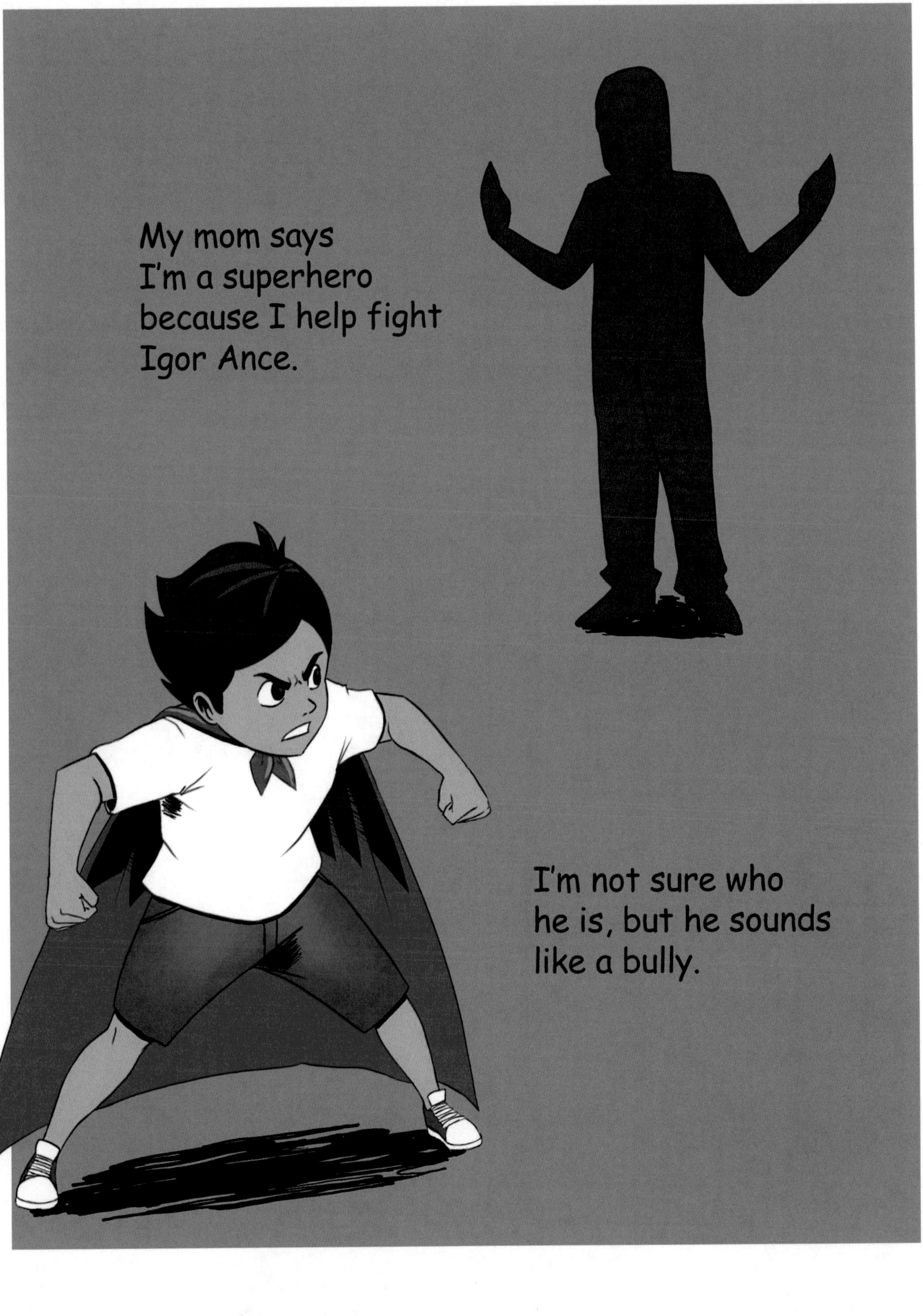
My mom says I'm a superhero because I help fight Igor Ance.
I'm not sure who he is, but he sounds like a bully.

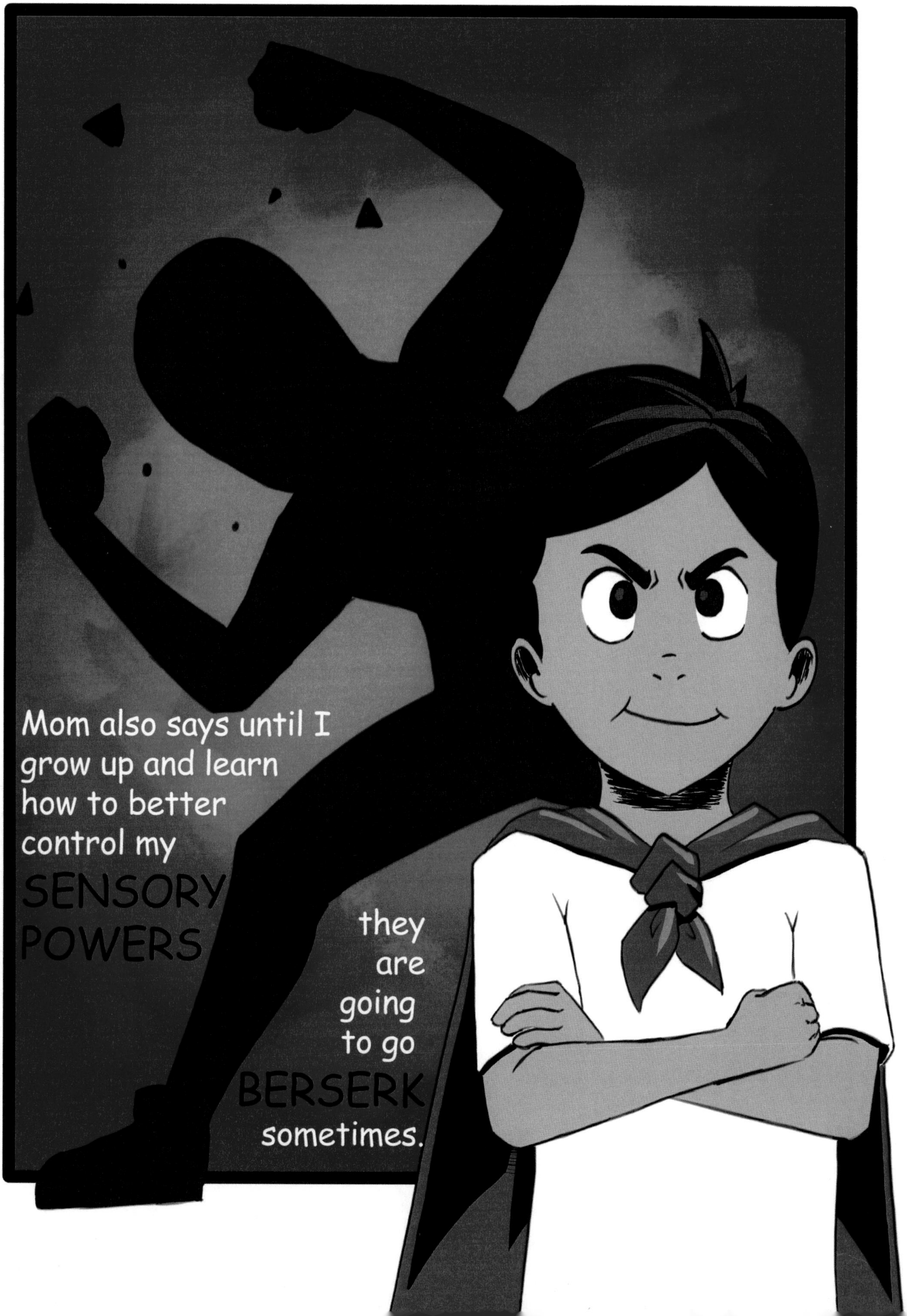
Mom also says until I grow up and learn how to better control my SENSORY POWERS
they are going to go BERSERK sometimes.

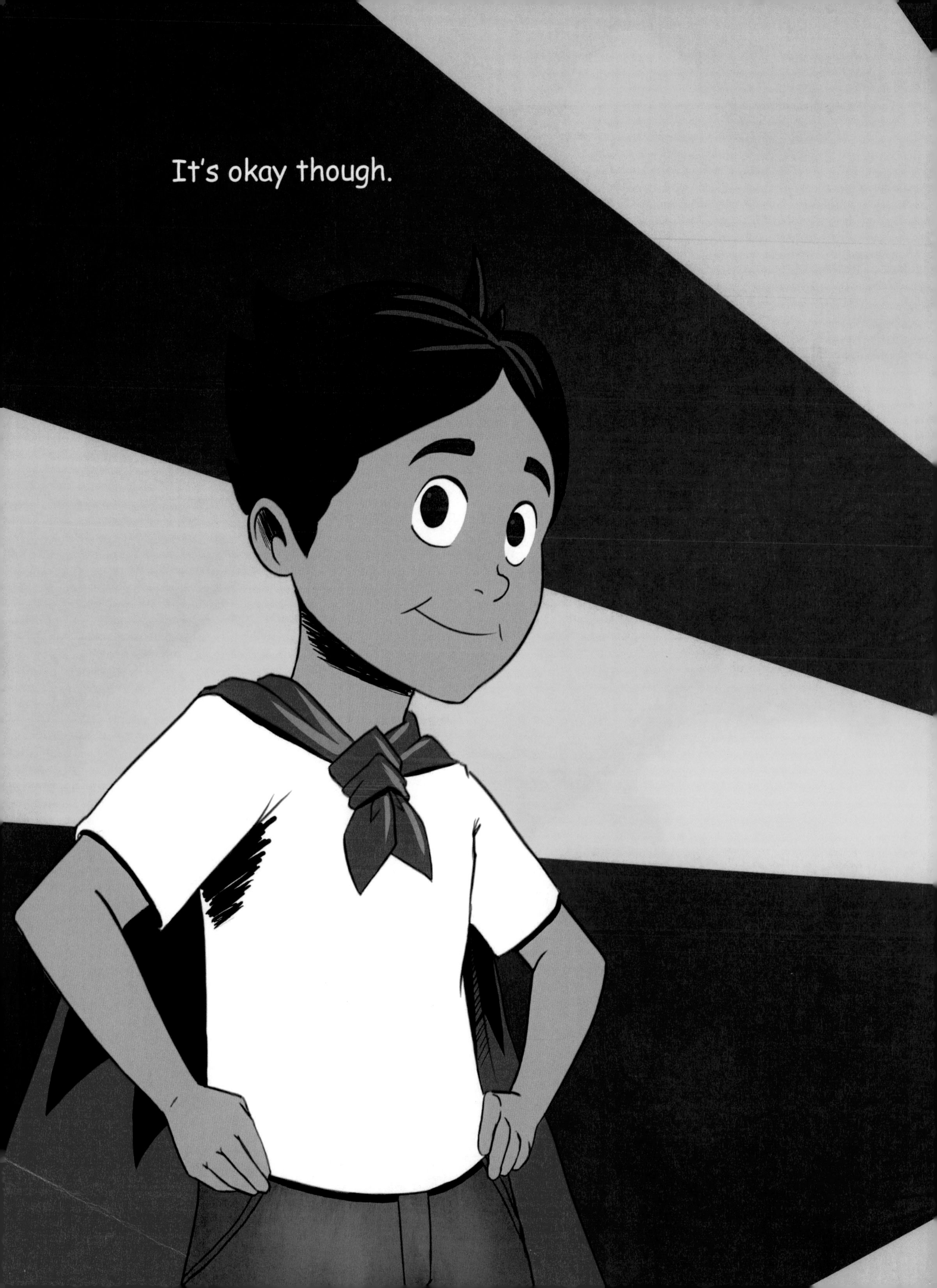
It's okay though.

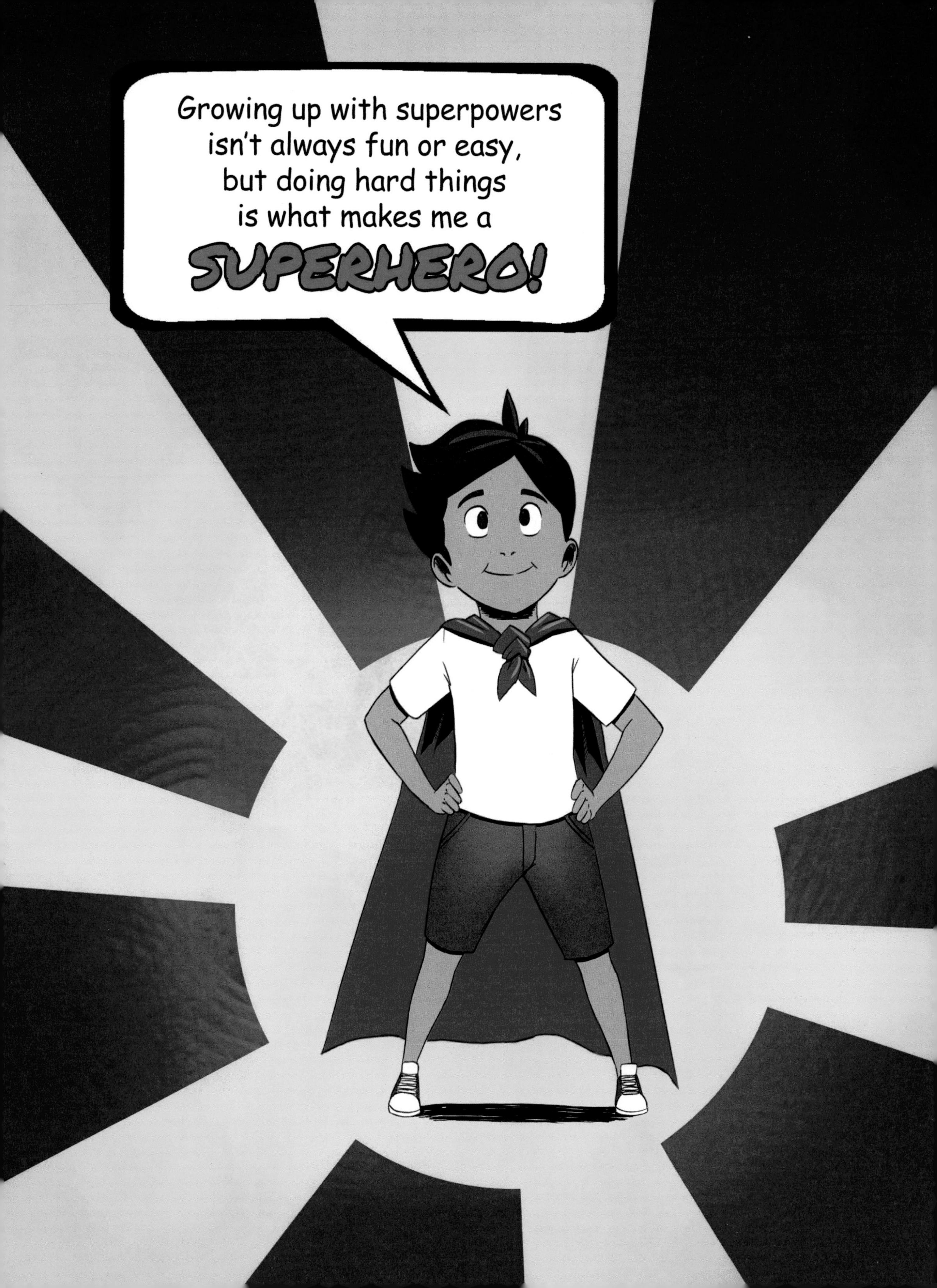
Growing up with superpowers isn't always fun or easy, but doing hard things is what makes me a SUPERHERO!

Sensory Processing Disorder, or SPD, is a real condition which affects 1 in 20 children. Although the acknowledgement of this disorder is growing, especially in children with Autism Spectrum Disorder, ignorance of the disorder and all that it entails is still very strong.

But, just like Clark said, if you have questions, ask. These superheroes will gladly share their secrets.


Learn more:

"About SPD." Sensory Processing Disorder - STAR Institute, www.spdstar.org/basic/about-spd.

Ahn, R. R., et al. "Prevalence of Parents Perceptions of sensory Processing Disorders Among Kindergarten Children." American Journal of Occupational Therapy, vol. 58, no. 3, Jan. 2004, pp. 287-293., doi:10.5014/ajot.58.3.287.


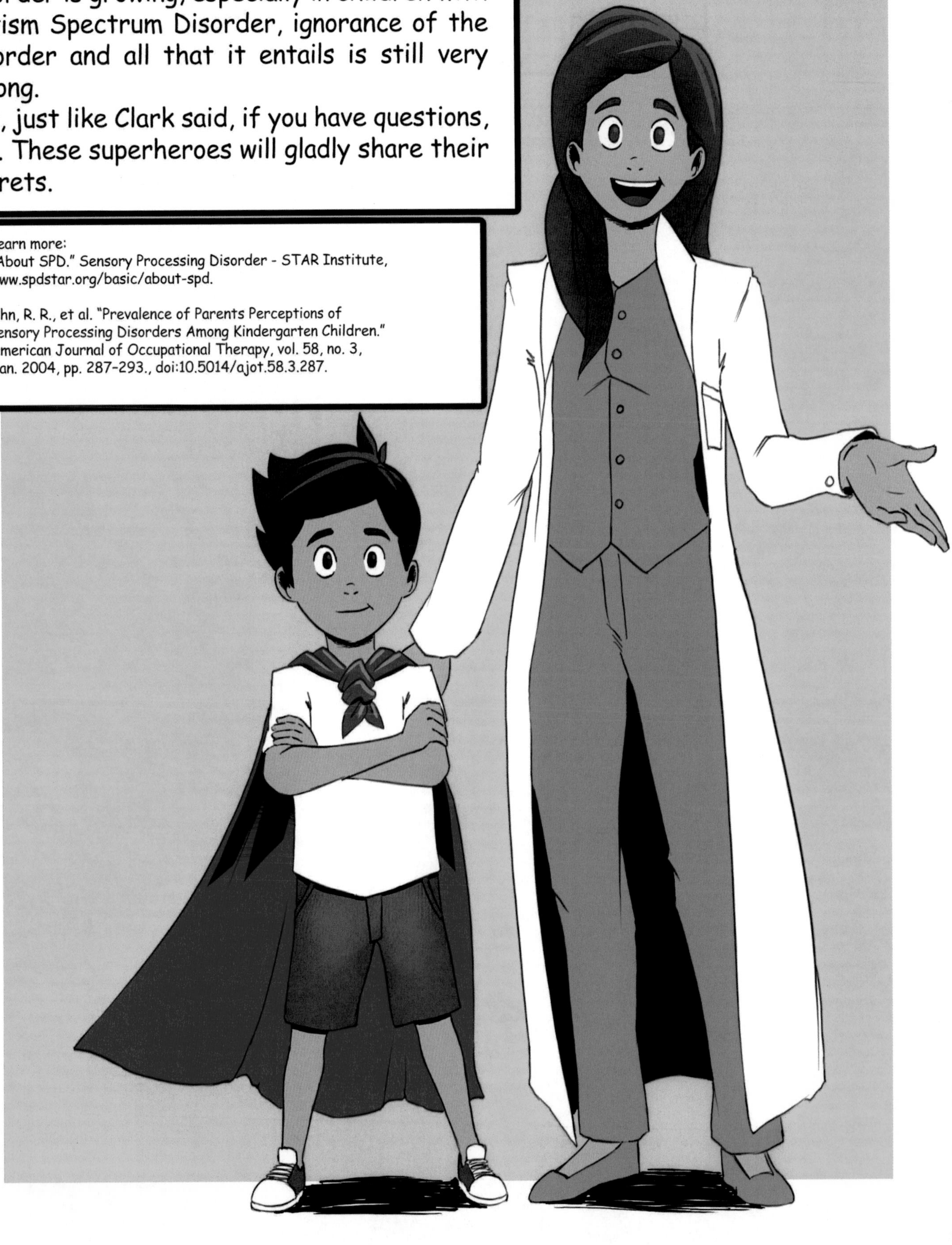

Made in the USA
Monee, IL
16 March 2022